P9-BZK-642

WELCOME TO AMERICA
BOOK 1

RED ONE™

WELCOME TO AMERICA BOOK 1

CREATED BY
XAVIER DORISON
& TERRY DODSON

XAVIER DORISON
SCRIPT

TERRY DODSON
PENCILS & COLORS

RACHEL DODSON
INKS

CLAYTON COWLES
LETTERS

RED ONE WELCOME TO AMERICA BOOK ONE HC. ISBN: 978-1-63215-400-2. First Printing. July 2015. Published by Image Comics, Inc. Office of publication: 2001 Center Street, 6th Floor, Berkeley, CA 94704.

красно одно (Red One) was the state function created by Comrade Iosif Vissarionovich Stalin during the 12th Communist Party Congress of the Soviet Union in April 1923 in honor of the female comrades who fell in the battle against the tyrannical capitalists during the Great Revolution. Red One is the eternal memory of their bodies, covered in the blood of sacrifice...

...and the last resort for Comrade First Secretary to help the Soviet citizenship in distress.

Comrade Red One is devoted to the Soviet people.

And only answers to Comrade First Secretary.

YOU MUST GO, MARY. IT'S ME THEY WANT...
IT'S NOT FAIR, ISHMAEL!
IS THAT WHAT YOU CALL HUMAN JUSTICE? IT'S NOT YOU THE POLICE SHOULD BE HOUNDING...
...BUT THEM!
YOU KNOW IT WON'T HAPPEN MY DARLING...THEY ARE REPROBATES AND BOLSHEVIKS...
THESE VERMIN HAVE MANAGED TO INFEST OUR OWN AMERICA. THE POLICE HAVE THEM IN THEIR PAY NOW! YOU MUST LEAVE ME, DAISY.
NO, ISHMAEL... WE ACTED TO SAVE OUR SOUL. WE HAVE NOTHING TO FEAR. SMILE WITH ME...
...GOD IS EXPECTING US.
The End
A MARVIN FILM CORPORATION PICTURE
BRAVO!
clap!
ENCORE!!!
clap!
clap!
The End
clap!
clap!
clap!
clap!
clap!
clap!
clap!

Clap!
Clap!
Clap!
Clap!
Clap!
LOS ANGELES,
MAY 1977.
THANK YOU! THANK YOU!
Lyn!
Clap!
Clap!
Clap!
Clap!
I *LOVE* YOU ALL!

THIS WAY, LYN...
ANOTHER SMILE!!!
LYN! LYN! THIS WAY!
YOU SHOULD GO NOW...
YOUR CAR IS WAITING. THE BACK *EXIT.*
LYN, ANOTHER ONE HERE.
"FROM BEHIND"?!!
DARLING, IF YOU WANT TO SEE ME ON ALL FOURS AGAIN IN ONE OF YOUR FILMS, I'D BETTER *NOT* DISAPPOINT MY FANS!

HOLD ON, LYN! THAT'S NOT IT...

THERE'S THE WITCH!
IT'S *HER!*
???!

STOP THE SHAME!
HEY...! WHO ARE THESE BASTARDS?!! WHAT DO THEY WANT?
WHAT I DO KNOW, BABE...
REPENT NOW!
LADY LUCK
NORTHERN COMFORT
SAVE YOUR
SAVE YOUR SELV
STOP THE SHAME!
"...THEY WON'T BE SIGNING UP FOR YOUR FAN CLUB!!"
LEAVE ME ALONE, JOE! I'M GOING TO SMASH THEIR PEASANT HEADS IN!!! IT'S MY PREMIERE THEY ARE RUINING!
YOU'LL HAVE OTHERS! COME ON, LET'S GO! THEY ARE CRAZY, LYN!
YOU SHOULDN'T BE HERE, MADAM! MOVE BACK!
MR. POLICEMAN... GOD HAS BROUGHT US HERE TO CREATE AN OBSTACLE TO PERVERSION AND TO SAVE THIS YOUNG WOMAN.
NOTHING WILL STAND IN OUR WAY.
MADAM, IF YOU HAVE NOT MOVED YOUR ASS FROM HERE WITHIN THREE SECONDS, YOU COULD BE THE POPE AND IT WOULDN'T STOP ME FROM DESTROYING YOU! IS THAT CLEAR?
DO WHATEVER YOUR CONSCIENCE TELLS YOU, MR. POLICEMAN...
ONE...
TWO...
THREE...
I MUST SAVE THIS YOUNG WOMAN, MR. POLICEMAN. THINK ABOUT WHAT SHE DOES...
THINK ABOUT WHAT SHE SHOWS TO HER MOTHER, HER FATHER, HER CHILDREN...
GIVE ME YOUR BATON! I'M GOING TO GET HER! I'M GOING TO GET HER!
SO, MR. POLICEMAN, CAN YOU SEE HER? DON'T YOU THINK THAT HER SOUL SHOULD BE SAVED...?
LET HER STOP SINNING AND REPENT, GOD WILL FORGIVE HER.
SHUT HER UP, DAMN IT!!
LET'S WITHDRAW INTO THE THEATER...
IT'S GOING TO GET CRAZY. WE'LL CLOSE THE GATES.
WHAT!
BLOODY COWARD! BASTARD! THEY ARE THE ONES WHO SHOULD BE BEHIND BARS! IT'S THEM!
SHUT UP! OR WE'LL PUT YOU IN THE SLAMMER TOO!
SAVE YOUR SOUL!
NOT HERE! NOT NOW!
REPENT
SOUL!

THEY WON'T GET AWAY WITH IT THAT EASILY!! I'LL STICK THEIR SIGNS WHERE THE SUN DOESN'T SHINE!
CALM DOWN, LYN, IT'S NO USE NOW! ON TOP OF THAT... LOOK AT **WHAT** THEY DID TO FUNNY BUNNY AND PINK LADY...
YOU KNOW WHAT **STATE** WE FOUND THEM IN? IT COULD HAVE BEEN WORSE FOR US.
WORSE?!!! I HAD TO SNEAK AWAY RIGHT AFTER MY **OWN FILM,** BOBBY!
I'LL MAKE THEM PAY FOR THIS, I SWEAR! JOE WANTED ME TO SHOOT THE REMAKE OF *"THE FARM"*...
I HATE THESE FUCKING COSTUME DRAMAS! I WANTED TO JET OFF TO THE BAHAMAS FOR A MONTH...BUT, YOU KNOW WHAT?
JUST TO PISS THEM OFF, I'M **GOING TO DO** HIS SHITTY FILM!! AND I'M GOING TO GET SO INTO IT THAT THESE PEASANTS WILL PREFER GETTING OFF WITH ME, RATHER THAN BAWLING WITH THAT FREAK!
HEY! **ARE YOU LISTENING** TO ME?
NO...
LOOK... ON THE BRIDGE.
HIM? TELL ME I'M DREAMING, BOBBY...
IT'S **NOT** A DREAM...
...IT'S A **NIGHTMARE!**

AAAAAAAAAAAHHHH!!
HIIIIIIIIIIII!!

HELP... HELP...GET OUT...
WELL HENRIETTE, IT LOOKS LIKE YOU HAVE GOT YOURSELF INTO TROUBLE AGAIN...
MY NAME'S LYN, SHIT...I'M BURNING HERE. GET ME OUT OF THIS...
NO.
AAAAAARGGH!!!
DON'T FORGET THE MAGIC WORD, HENRIETTE... I'M GOING TO HAVE TO WASH YOUR MOUTH OUT WITH SOAP, YOU'RE SO RUDE! YOUR TEACHER HAS TOLD ME SOME AWFUL THINGS.
MY HAND!!! MY HAND...
I'M SURE YOU UNDERSTAND THAT YOU NEED SOME GOOD MANNERS... DON'T YOU?
AAAAH... AAAHH
GOOD MANNERS... YES...WHATEVER YOU LIKE...BUT GET ME OUT OF HERE! I BEG YOU! I'LL DO WHATEVER YOU TELL ME!
I...I CAN DO LOADS OF THINGS... INCREDIBLE...
WILL YOU BE A GOOD GIRL?
YES, YES...
YOU'LL PUT ALL THAT FORNICATION BEHIND YOU?
YES...I SWEAR...NO MORE...
COME BACK, YOU BASTARD! COME BACK!!
TSK... TSK...LIAR ONCE...
...LIAR ALWAYS...

*SOVIET SPECIAL FORCES
**SOVIET ATTACK HELICOPTER

...MINE IS ALL WET.
. . .
TAKE MINE!
NO, MINE!
THIS ONE!
MINE!

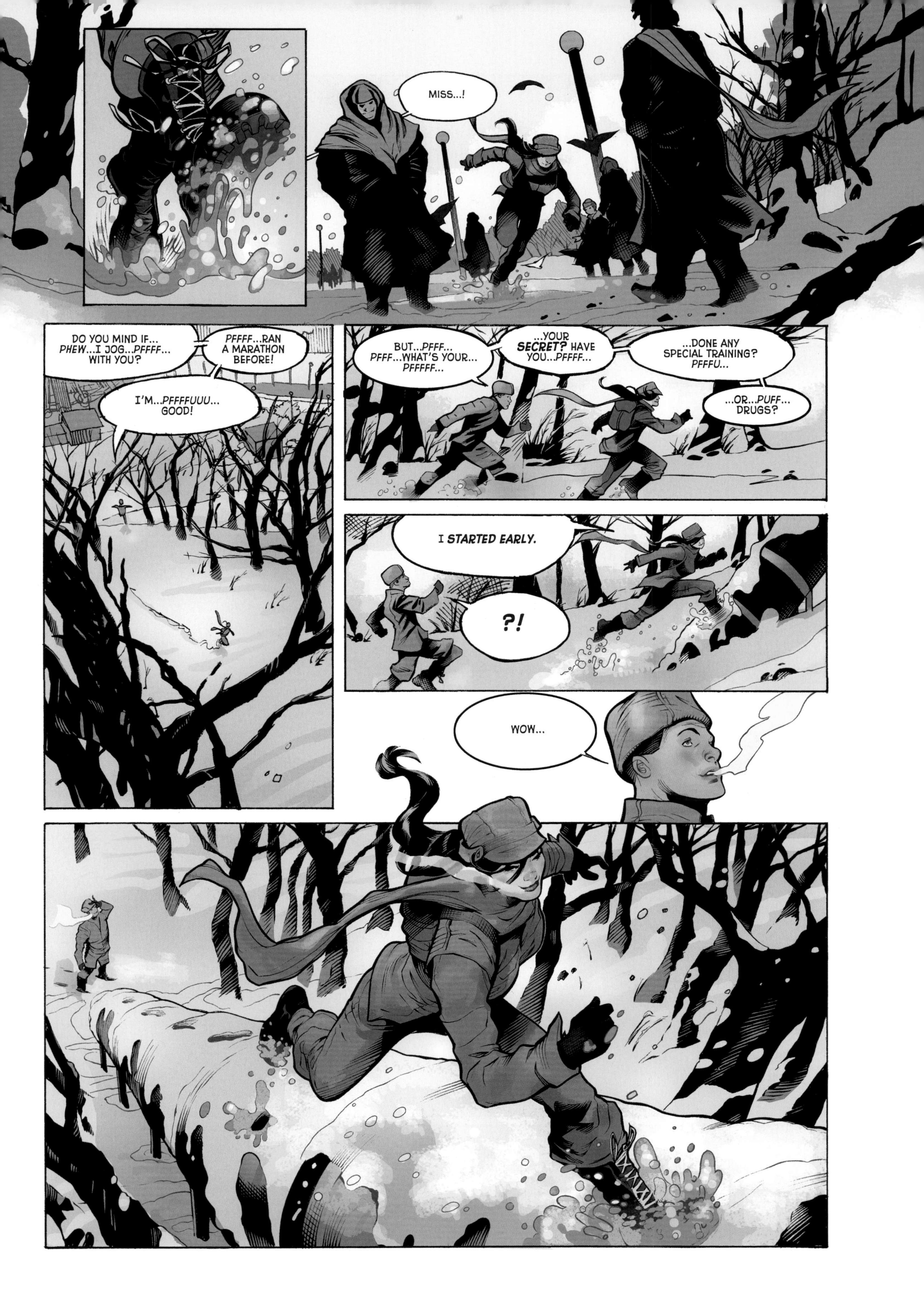

MISS...!
DO YOU MIND IF... *PHEW*...I JOG...*PFFFF*... WITH YOU?
PFFFF...RAN A MARATHON BEFORE!
I'M...*PFFFFUUU*... GOOD!
BUT...*PFFF*... *PFFF*...WHAT'S YOUR... *PFFFFF*...
...YOUR **SECRET?** HAVE YOU...*PFFFF*...
...DONE ANY SPECIAL TRAINING? *PFFFU*...
...OR...*PUFF*... DRUGS?
I **STARTED EARLY.**
?!
WOW...

YOU ARE NOT SUPPOSED TO TALK TO THE SOLDIERS.
ALL MY CLOTHES WERE STILL IN THE WASH AND I NEEDED A...
VERA... NOT TO ME...
OKAY, GEORG! OKAY...THEY WERE CUTE. AND HONESTLY, IF I HADN'T SET UP A MEETING WITH YOU...
HERE, THIS IS FOR YOU.
WHAT IS IT?
TRABANT.
BRAND NEW.
COMRADE FIRST SECRETARY WANTED ME TO GIVE YOU THIS GIFT. HE LOVED YOUR PERFORMANCES IN KABUL...IT COULD GET DICEY THERE AGAIN...HE WANTS TO SEND YOU BACK.
I DON'T REALLY FEEL LIKE GOING BACK...AND I DRIVE A MOTORCYCLE, GEORG.
YOU COULDN'T TELL HIM THAT I'D PREFER A CASE OF VODKA AND THREE DAYS TO CRASH OUT, COULD YOU?
I'LL SEE WHAT I CAN DO ABOUT THE VODKA...
YOU'RE ON LEAVE, VERA...BUT YOU MUST STAY NEAR A TELEPHONE.
YOU CAN DRIVE A CAR OR A MOTORCYCLE IF YOU LIKE...
"...BUT YOU DON'T PICK THE DESTINATION."

MIRCO
NEXT.
DO YOU KNOW IF HE HAS ANY MORE CANNED PEARS?
THAT WOULD BE TOO GOOD TO BE TRUE! THAT THIEF CLAIMS HE HAS NEVER HAD ANY! AND THAT FOR HIM TO GET ANY, THE PARTY WOULD HAVE TO WORK MIRACLES!
IT'S A SHAME HE'S NOT A BELIEVER...
NEXT.
HELLO, I NEED A KILO OF SUGAR, TWO KILOS OF FLOUR, TWO OF RICE AND...CANNED PEARS?
I HAVE SAUSAGES WITH BEANS OR BEANS WITH SAUSAGES! THAT'S ALL.
YOU'VE GOT YOUR DATES MIXED UP, DARLING! IT'S NOT CHRISTMAS!
MAYBE IT IS...
VERY FRESH, STRAIGHT FROM KABUL... TEMPTED?
OH THANK YOU, BUT HOW...
CHRISTMAS! THE PARTY JUST CHANGED THE DATE.

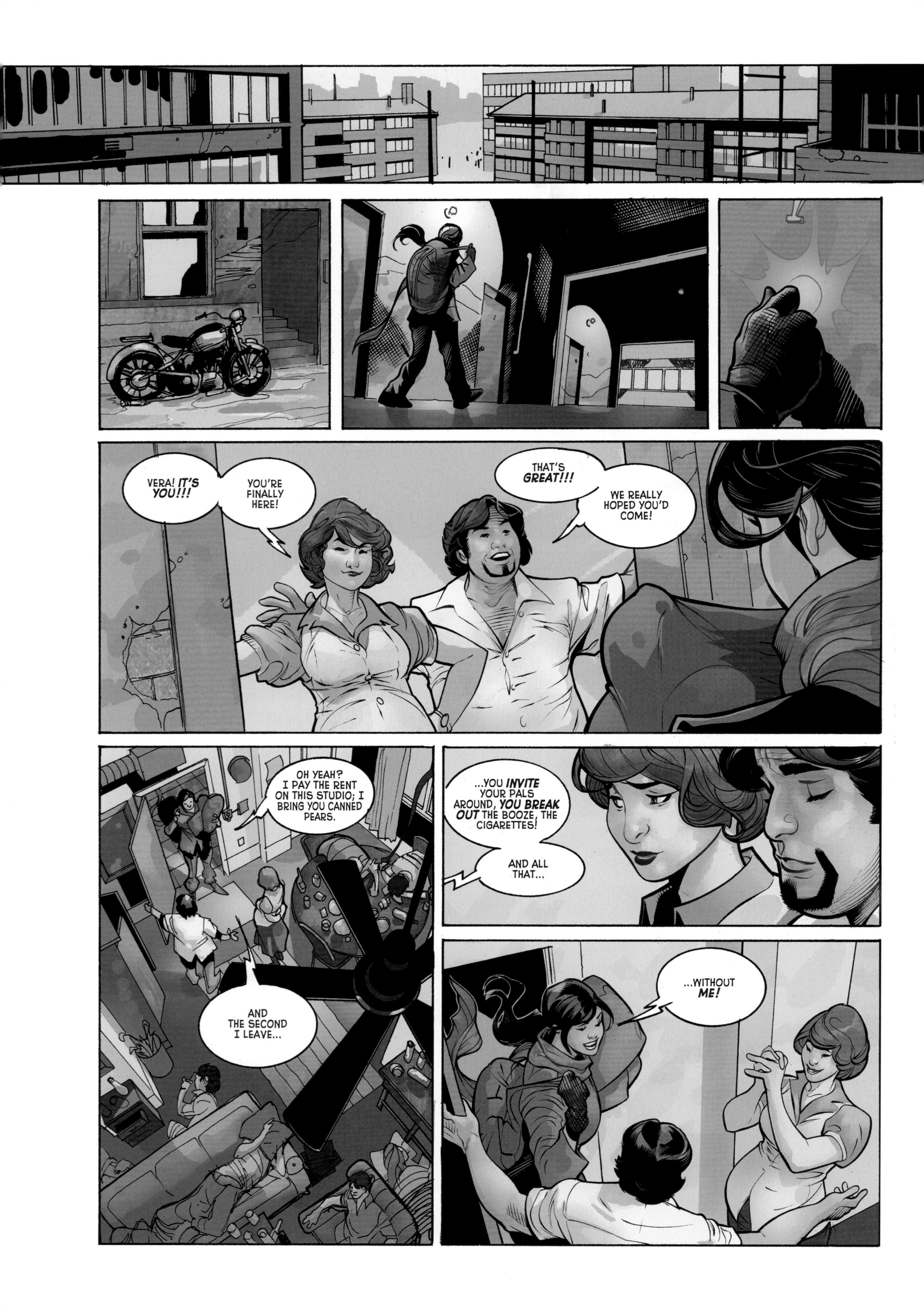
VERA! IT'S YOU!!!
YOU'RE FINALLY HERE!
THAT'S GREAT!!!
WE REALLY HOPED YOU'D COME!
OH YEAH? I PAY THE RENT ON THIS STUDIO; I BRING YOU CANNED PEARS.
AND THE SECOND I LEAVE...
...YOU INVITE YOUR PALS AROUND, YOU BREAK OUT THE BOOZE, THE CIGARETTES!
AND ALL THAT...
...WITHOUT ME!

Riiiiiiing...
Riiiiiiing
Riiiiiiing...
Riiiiiiing
Riiiiiiing...
Riiiiiiing
HMMM... LEAVE IT, VERA... LET IT RING. WE'RE SO COZY HERE...
I KNOW...
IT'S SIX O'CLOCK...WHAT SORT OF MORON PHONES AT THIS TIME IN THE MORNING...?
Riiiiiiing...
Riiiiiiing
VERA, IT'S GEORG. GENERAL LEONISEV WANTS TO SEE YOU.
FINE.
TOMORROW.
RIGHT AWAY. HE'S GOT ORDERS FOR YOU. FROM COMRADE BREZHNEV.
THAT'S LESS FINE.
YOUR LEAVE HAS BEEN CANCELLED. YOU'RE OFF AGAIN.
ANGOLA? AFGHANISTAN? LAOS? MOZAMBIQUE?
THE UNITED STATES.
?!!!

TELL ME, VERA, WHAT DO YOU THINK OF "BATMAN"?
WHO IS THAT?
A FICTIONAL CHARACTER. LIKE SPIDER-MAN OR SUPERMAN...
AMERICANS BLESSED WITH VARIOUS MAGICAL POWERS WHO FIGHT INJUSTICE AND CRIME. IN THE U.S., THEY MAKE COMICS ABOUT THEM, AND EVEN FILMS. THEY ARE LITERALLY WORSHIPPED.
SO AMERICANS STILL BELIEVE IN FAIRY TALES?
THE FAIRY TALE ISN'T IMPORTANT. WHAT MATTERS VERA, IS THAT THE AMERICANS WANT TO BELIEVE IT...AND THAT SOMEONE HAS GRANTED THEIR WISHES.
WITH A FARMER?
A "CARPENTER"... WELL, AT LEAST THAT'S WHAT THEY'VE CALLED HIM.

HANG ON...JUST SO WE'RE CLEAR...THE AMERICANS SEE THIS PSYCHOPATH AS A "SUPERHERO"?
...HMM...
LET'S JUST SAY THAT MOST AMERICANS DON'T GIVE A DAMN, THAT A GOOD NUMBER WOULD BE MORE THAN HAPPY...
...TO SEE HIM FRY ON THE ELECTRIC CHAIR...
BUT, THERE'S ANOTHER GROUP...
...THAT THINK THAT THIS "CARPENTER"...
...IS CLEANING UP THE UNITED STATES.
GENERAL...HOW DOES ALL OF THIS CONCERN US?
IT CONCERNS YOU, BECAUSE COMRADE BREZHNEV SAYS SO, VERA.
CALM DOWN, GEORG, CALM DOWN... I UNDERSTAND OUR COMRADE'S QUESTION.
MY DEAR, WHAT YOU HAVE TO UNDERSTAND, IS THAT THE STORIES A SOCIETY HOLDS IN THE HIGHEST REGARD ALWAYS END UP INFLUENCING THEIR POLITICAL AFFAIRS...
...AND WE WOULD PREFER IT IF THESE STORIES PUT US IN A GOOD LIGHT.
COMRADE BREZHNEV WANTS THE AMERICANS SINGING "PEACE & LOVE" INSTEAD OF "DEATH TO COMMIES AND GAYS"...
...FOR THEM TO SEE THEMSELVES MORE AS BOB MARLEY THAN JOHN WAYNE.
JOHN WHO?

*BILATERAL NUCLEAR DISARMAMENT AGREEMENT.

...IT'S YOU!
PLEASE THANK COMRADE BREZHNEV FOR ME, BUT HE MUST HAVE MADE A MISTAKE. I LEARNED ENGLISH BECAUSE MY JOB IS SEARCH AND RESCUE. BUT I DON'T KNOW ANYTHING ABOUT "UNDERCOVER" MISSIONS...
LEAST OF ALL IN THE STATES!
IT'S IN CALIFORNIA, VERA!
THE SUPERMARKETS!
THE PALM TREES!
THE HAMBURGERS!
THE BIG FAST BIKES!
WHAT DO YOU WANT ME TO DO ABOUT IT?
I'VE GOT NOTHING TO DO OVER THERE!
YES, YOU HAVE, COMRADE.
SAY, GEORG...
BAM
TELL ME, GEORG...DO YOU THINK YOU COULD SET UP A DINNER FOR ME WITH HER, BEFORE SHE LEAVES? I'M SURE SHE HAS CERTAIN "TALENTS" SHE COULD PUT TO GOOD USE...
OF ALL THE TALENTS SHE HAS, THE ONE YOU'RE ASKING ME FOR...IS THE ONLY ONE SHE'S ALWAYS REFUSED TO USE FOR THE PARTY.
AH YES... I UNDERSTAND BREZHNEV BETTER NOW...
HUM...WHAT DO YOU UNDERSTAND, MY GENERAL?
WHY HE'S LETTING HER GO SO FAR AWAY FROM HIM.

ALREADY? BUT YOU'VE ONLY JUST GOT HERE!
CAN'T IT WAIT TWO OR THREE DAYS? YOU'RE SUPPOSED TO HAVE TWO WEEKS!
COME ON...AT LEAST STAY TODAY. I'VE MADE YOU YOUR FAVORITE LATKAS!
I'VE INVITED LYBLIN AND VOLKO OVER THIS AFTERNOON TO CELEBRATE YOU COMING BACK AGAIN.
I KNOW THAT PEOPLE AREN'T FALLING OVER THEMSELVES TO GO TO SIBERIA, BUT YOU'RE NOT THE ONLY ENGINEER IN THIS FACTORY ARE YOU?
I PROMISE I'LL DO EVERYTHING I CAN TO COME BACK AS QUICKLY AS POSSIBLE...
IT'S JUST THAT...
THE BABY'S DUE SOON AND WE WERE HOPING IT'D BE KIND OF OUR CHILD...ALL THREE OF US.
SINCE YOU'VE KNOWN ME ALL THIS TIME, YOU SHOULD KNOW, MY LOVES...
...NOT TO COUNT ON ME.

WHAT ARE YOU DOING WITH A JACKET...?
YOU'RE GOING TO CA-LI-FOR-NIA!! IT'S GOING TO BE 90° IN THE SHADE!!
HOW DO YOU EXPECT ME TO KNOW THAT?!
THAT FUCKING COUNTRY IS BETWEEN THE PACIFIC AND THE ATLANTIC! THAT'S ALL I KNOW ABOUT IT!
WHAT ABOUT LUGGAGE? YOU NEED ENOUGH FOR AT LEAST SIX MONTHS...HAVEN'T YOU GOT ANYTHING ELSE?
MY WHOLE LIFE IS IN THERE!
GEORG... YOU COULD HAVE HAD THE SPETSNAZ, THE BLACK BERETS, OR THE B.R.K... WHY ME?
BECAUSE I'VE INVESTED 21 YEARS OF MY LIFE IN YOU...
...THE LONGEST COMMANDO TRAINING PROGRAMME EVER PUT IN PLACE BY THE RED ARMY...AND, BY A LOOOOOONG WAY...YOU'RE THE BEST SOLDIER THE U.S.S.R. HAS GOT!
"A GOOD SOLDIER IS ONE WHO HAS A PASSION FOR HIS MISSION." YOU TAUGHT ME THAT.
"YOUR LIFE IS NOT DRIVEN BY PLEASURE." THAT'S WHAT I TRIED TO TEACH YOU! FIRST AND FOREMOST YOU ARE A CITIZEN OF THE SOVIET UNION...
"AND VERA YELNIKOV SECOND." I KNOW!
TAKE THE DEVICE ON THE SEAT.
WHAT IS IT?
IN THE STATES, IT WILL BE THE EPITOME OF TECHNOLOGY...
...THE "WALKMAN".
ON THE FACE OF IT, IT PLAYS CASSETTES. AND I'VE RECORDED MY INSTRUCTIONS ONTO ONE FOR YOU...BUT, IN ACTUAL FACT, IT IS A TWO-WAY RADIO. YOUR ONLY LINK WITH YOUR CONTACT IN LOS ANGELES.
HE CALLS YOU. HE MAKES THE DECISIONS. YOU OBEY. THE ONLY THING YOU HAVE TO DO IS TO FOLLOW HIS INSTRUCTIONS. DON'T THINK ABOUT IT AND EVERYTHING WILL GO FINE.
AND WHAT IF I WANT TO KNOW HOW MASHA AND ALYOSHA ARE DOING?
THAT IS NOT PART OF THE PLAN.
GEORG... WHY ME?
I THOUGHT I'D ALREADY TOLD YOU.
NO. YOU'VE JUST GIVEN ME THE USUAL BULLSHIT...

I'M GETTING OLD, VERA...
I'M TIRED OF RISKING MY NECK. IF THIS OPERATION WORKS, THEY'VE PROMISED I CAN RETIRE.
THERE YOU ARE, YOU SEE! YOU KNOW HOW TO MOTIVATE ME WHEN YOU WANT TO!
THIS CASSETTE CONTAINS YOUR FINAL INSTRUCTIONS.
IN A FEW HOURS' TIME, YOU WILL HAVE A NEW IDENTITY. YOU ARE A POOR GIRL FROM ALABAMA...THAT'S RIGHT, WE COULDN'T FIND ANY MORE OF A MISFIT!
YOU ONLY HAVE $400 IN YOUR POCKET. ANY MORE WOULD SEEM LIKE TOO MUCH.
YOUR PRIORITY ON ARRIVAL IS TO FIND A JOB. IN THIS COUNTRY, BEING OUT OF WORK IS SUSPICIOUS...
AS SOON AS YOUR PLANE LANDS, GO STRAIGHT TO LEW GARNER'S HOME AT 1106 CARLYLE AVE, SANTA MONICA. HE NEEDS A DRIVER FOR A FEW MONTHS. IT MUST BE YOU.
AND DON'T TRY TO UNDERSTAND "WHY HIM?"!! WE HAVE OUR REASONS.
YOU WILL ARRIVE AT DAWN. GARNER IS GOING TO ORDER A TAXI TO GET TO WORK AND SEE SOME CANDIDATES FOR THE JOB THERE... SEE HIM BEFORE THAT.
YOUR COMBAT GEAR WILL BE DELIVERED DIRECTLY TO YOU BY YOUR CONTACT, BUT LATER.
TAKE GOOD CARE OF YOURSELF, VERA, AND GET READY TO BECOME...
...AN AMERICAN.

HMM...YOU...DON'T YOU LIKE FLYING? AIR SICKNESS, MAYBE?
I HATE BEING STUCK IN A CLOSED BOX... EVEN AT 30,000 FEET...
I UNDERSTAND. I'M THE SAME! SO, WHEN I GET STRESSED, I'VE GOT INTO THE HABIT OF USING SHAKRA MEDITATION. HAVE YOU HEARD OF IT?
WELL, I HAVE ANOTHER THING THAT RELAXES ME. INVOLVING SOMEONE ELSE.
COULD YOU MAYBE...DO ME A FAVOR?
!!!!
IF... IF I CAN BE OF ASSISTANCE.
OCCUPIED
DINER
KING
7's
ce cream
"IT ALL SEEMS TO BE IN ORDER, MA'AM."
ALABAMA JANE...
PASSPORTS
UNITED STATES
...WELCOME TO CALIFORNIA.

THIS IS THE LAND OF CARS. YOU'LL SEE; THEY LOVE THEM SO MUCH THEY'VE ALMOST FORGOTTEN HOW TO PUT ONE FOOT IN FRONT OF THE OTHER.
MEL'S AUTOS
YOU HAVE ONE HOUR TO FIND YOURSELF A CAR AND TO GET TO YOUR MEETING.
CHEVROLET 1970...NO A.C., BUT THE WINDOWS OPEN FINE! REAL WOOD STEERING WHEEL, PURE LEATHERETTE SEATS... ELEGANCE ITSELF! IT'LL FIT YOU LIKE A GLOVE!
I WON'T BOTHER YOU WITH THE MOTOR...
I KNOW ENGINES AND WOMEN DON'T GO WELL TOGETHER...
OF COURSE... US WOMEN, WE PREFER BROOMS AND SAUCEPANS...
DEAL!
AND WHAT ABOUT THAT MOTORBIKE THERE?
THAT PIECE OF JUNK?
OH! OH! NO, TAKE THE CHEVROLET, LITTLE LADY!
IF NOT, I'VE GOT OTHER MOTORBIKES, SUZUKIS! BUT THAT ONE IS THOROUGHLY THRASHED, FROM THE HANDLEBARS TO THE TIRES!
ARE YOU SURE? THIS PILE OF SCRAP IS REALLY WORTH NOTHING?
NO-THING.
SO, IF I OFFERED YOU $200 WITH 2 SPARK PLUGS, A 4-STROKE CARBURETOR, TWO BRAKE PADS, AND 20 MINUTES IN YOUR GARAGE THROWN IN... YOU'D THANK ME?
???!...IF YOU WANT, LITTLE LADY, BUT I DON'T KNOW ANYBODY WHO COULD REPAIR THIS PILE OF CRAP!
...NO, ME NEITHER.
BRROOOM BRROOOM
?!!!!...
GARAGE WORK

HOW DO YOU FANCY MISSING YOUR NEXT CUSTOMER?
?!!
WITH YOU?
IN A HEARTBEAT...BUT I'VE GOT AN APPOINTMENT! MY CAB'S HIRED...
200 DOLLARS...
WILL THAT COVER THE CANCELLATION CHARGES?
BETTY, I AM A REASONABLE WOMAN!
OF COURSE THE CARPENTER IS A REAL MAN...
...IN THE SAME WAY THAT JESUS MADE HIMSELF HUMAN TO SAVE US!
DO YOU THINK THAT THE CARPENTER IS AT RISK OF MEETING A SIMILAR END TO CHRIST?
I BELIEVE THAT HE WILL SUCCEED, LIKE HIM.
WHAT THE HELL AM I DOING, JOE?!! I'M TRYING TO TIE MY $*@€ LACES!
BUT HE IS TAKING A LOT OF RISKS. TO BE HONEST, BETTY, TO SAVE HIS COUNTRY THE WAY HE IS DOING, WHO AMONG US WOULD BE READY TO RISK THEIR LIFE AGAINST CRIMINALS?
I'M WAITING FOR A FUCKING TAXI! WHAT DO YOU WANT ME TO SAY? I'M SURE THEY GET A BONUS FOR TURNING UP LATE!
HE IS A ROLE MODEL. AND I CALL ON ALL TRUE AMERICANS TO FOLLOW HIM SO THAT WE CAN CLEANSE OUR COUNTRY OF THE COMMUNISTS AND PERVERTS WHO ARE DESTROYING IT!

AND IT IS PRIMARILY OUR YOUNG PEOPLE WE MUST DEPEND ON TO LEAD THE FIGHT!
YOU KNOW, BETTY, THE COMMUNISTS TEACH THEIR CHILDREN HOW TO HANDLE A GRENADE OR A GUN FROM THE AGE OF FIVE! AND EVEN HOW TO PLANT MINES!
...WHY AREN'T WE DOING THE SAME??
COME ON...IT'S UP TO YOU CHILDREN!
YESSSS I'M GOING TO GET A FUCKING DRIVER! AND I'LL BE WITH YOU ON TIME...AND BANKRUPT!!
TO THE CARPENTER WHO IS PURIFYING OUR COUNTRY...KEEP US UNIIIITEDD...
YOU, WHO PROTECT AMERI... ZZZT!
BRAF
SHUT THE HELL UP YOU BRATS!
DING-DONG
I DO NOT BUY MAGAZINES, I DO NOT NEED NEW WINDOWS, I DO NOT SIGN PETITIONS, AND KRISHNA CAN GO TO HELL.
SO, BEAT IT.
I'M HERE ABOUT THE AD.
?!

DO YOU KNOW HOW TO COOK?
NO.
DO YOU HAVE ANY REFERENCES?
NO.
DO YOU AT LEAST HAVE A DRIVER'S LICENSE?
NOPE.
WELL THEN, LADY, WHAT, IN THAT THING YOU CALL A BRAIN, MAKES YOU THINK YOU WILL GET THE JOB???!!!
MY PERSONALITY?
VLAM!!
I AM 73 YEARS OLD, LITTLE GIRL! YOU KNOW WHERE YOU CAN STICK YOUR ASSETS AND YOUR PERSONALITY?!!!
Riiiing... Riiiing...
DAMMIT, JOE! CALLING EVERY TWO MINUTES IS NOT GOING TO MAKE THE $*$** TAXI COME ANY FASTER!
I KNOW THAT SHOOTING IS STARTING!! WHAT DO YOU WANT ME TO DO? COME BY BICYCLE?!
I HAVE A MOTORCYCLE.
I HOPE YOU DRIVE SLOWLY.

I SAID... SLOWLY!!
CLOSE YOUR EYES! YOU'LL FEEL BETTER!
NOW WHICH WAY?
TAKE THE NEXT RIGHT...
Palm Vis
Hollywood Blvd 3/4 Burbank
RED LIGHT!!!
THERE'S NO ONE AROUND!
WHERE DO I GO NOW?
STRAIGHT AHEAD! WAGNER STUDIOS! SHOOTING STARTS IN ONE MINUTE!
CAN'T THEY START WITHOUT YOU?
I'M THE DIRECTOR!
THIS IS JUST WHAT WE NEED! IT'S HAINSLEY! WITH ALL HIS BLAH BLAH, PAPERWORK, OPENING THE GATE, IT'S GOING TO TAKE AT LEAST TEN MINUTES!
DOES HE KNOW YOU?
HE SEES ME EVERY DAY!
GIVE HIM A BIG SMILE.
UHH... YES...WHY?
BECAUSE WE'RE NOT STOPPING.
????

AAAAAAAAAAAAAAAAAAAAAAAAHH!
DAMN!!!! WHERE DID YOU LEARN TO DO THAT????!!!
GIRL SCOUTS.
HOW DID YOU HURT YOUR ARM?
SKIING?
CAR ACCIDENT?
I FAILED TO KILL MYSELF.
?!
CLOSED SET THE FARM
AND I'D LIKE TO WAIT A WHILE BEFORE TRYING AGAIN! SO TONIGHT, FIND OUT WHERE THE BRAKES ARE!
YOU'RE THE BOSS...
NOT SO FAST! NO ONE SAID THAT YOU WERE HIRED.

LEW, YOU KNOW HOW MUCH THIS SET COSTS? THE WHOLE CREW IS WAITING FOR YOU! BE LATE ONE MORE TIME, AND I WILL THROW YOU IN CEMENT AND SINK YOU IN THE RIVER.
AND YOU WILL SINK YOUR FILM AT THE SAME TIME! AT LEAST I'D GET A VACATION!
LEW
WHILE YOU'RE WAITING FOR YOUR VACATION, ARE YOU GOING TO SHOOT, YES OR NO?
FOXY'S BEEN KEEPING THEM UP FOR AN HOUR! ANY LONGER AND SHE'LL GET BLISTERS!
YEEEESSSS I'M SHOOTING! IF THOSE TWO STUDS ARE READY!
PLACES, EVERYONE!
LET'S FINISH SCENE 18: "DAISY IS SAVED BY TWO NEIGHBORS WHO HAVE COME OVER TO KEEP HER SPIRITS UP."
YOU TWO, START NICE AND SLOW. TAKE YOUR TIME. YOU SEE THAT SHE'S NOT GETTING ENOUGH, SO YOU REALLY PUT IT TO HER. OKAY?
OKAY, LEW.
Tiiiit... Tiiiit
YOUR EQUIPMENT IS READY, MY DARLING. GO TO 709B NORTH LA BREA AVENUE. NOW.
SCENE 12, TAKE 1. CAMERA
QUIET ON THE SET.
I'M COMING.
ACTION!
WOW...

WAIT!
YOU THINK YOU CAN COME AND GO JUST LIKE THAT?!! WHAT DO YOU THINK THIS BARRIER IS FOR? IT'S NOT FOR DOGS!
IT'S FOR PEOPLE THAT YOU DON'T KNOW! AND YOU KNOW LEW GARNER? AND NOW YOU KNOW ME, TOO.
HEY THERE! GET OFF OF YOUR BIKE IMMEDIATELY OR...
IT'S ALL RIGHT, HAINSLEY.
?!
THE YOUNG LADY IS WITH ME.
WELL IN THAT CASE...AS YOU LIKE, MR. JONES.
NOW THAT THEY ARE FILMING, I FINALLY HAVE SOME TIME TO MYSELF.
CAN I OFFER YOU A DRINK? MISS...?
I'M IN A HURRY.
AH! AH! THANK YOU! IT'S BEEN A LONG TIME SINCE SOMEONE HAS TURNED ME DOWN!! BUT, TELL ME. DO YOU KNOW WHO I AM?
NO, SHOULD I?
JOE JONES. I AM THE PRODUCER FOR "THE FARM". THE SHOOT, THE SOUND STAGE, THE CREW. IT'S ALL ME!
AH, YES. YOU'RE THE ONE WHO MAKES THE PEOPLE PAY TO TAKE PART. IS IT EXPENSIVE FOR THEM?
YOU... YOU'RE JOKING, RIGHT?
NO, WHY?
THEY DON'T PAY, I DO!
NOOOO? REALLY?
I AM GOING TO THROW A PARTY FOR THE CREW, TO THANK THEM FOR GOING AHEAD WITH THE SHOOT AFTER WHAT HAPPENED TO CRYSTAL.
DO YOU WANT TO COME?
ONLY IF YOU INVITE MY BOSS, AND IF THERE WILL BE VODKA.
I WILL HAVE FOUNTAINS OF IT! AND MISS, ARE YOU SURE ABOUT LEW? HE'S THE BIGGEST DUD IN THE INDUSTRY!

CAN I HELP YOU, MISS?
I... I WOULD LIKE TO REPAIR MY TELEVISION.
CLOSED
ARE YOU VERA YELNIKOV?
IS IT THAT OBVIOUS?
NO ONE GETS THEIR TELEVISION REPAIRED IN THIS COUNTRY!!! THEY JUST THROW THEM OUT! AND THEN THEY BUY A NEW ONE!
SORRY.
CLOSED
YOU NEED TO GET UP TO SPEED QUICKLY OR ELSE YOU'RE GOING TO GET ME IN A SHITLOAD OF TROUBLE!
DID IT TAKE YOU A LONG TIME TO LEARN EVERYTHING HERE?
I WAS READY BEFORE I CAME. READING, DOCUMENTATION, CLASSES, ETC. BUT DON'T WORRY, YOU COULDN'T HAVE DONE IT AS QUICKLY AS I DID.
OH YEAH?
I HAVE AN IQ OF 245.
OOH...

BUT I COULD INITIATE YOU TO THE LOCAL CUSTOMS. FOR EXAMPLE, DO YOU WANT TO COME TO THE MOVIES WITH ME ON FRIDAY NIGHT?
THEY'RE SHOWING A NEW SCI-FI FLICK, STAR WARS. NO ONE WILL BOTHER US. I DON'T THINK IT WILL HAVE MUCH SUCCESS, THE MOVIE THEATRE WILL BE EMPTY.
BEFORE WE GO ON A DATE, DON'T YOU HAVE SOME PRESENTS FOR ME FROM MOSCOW?
IT JUST ARRIVED THIS MORNING. THEY ARE SPOILING YOU! TAKE OFF YOUR CLOTHES AND TRY IT ON.
HERE?
PFFFF! I'VE SEEN OTHERS, YOU KNOW.
BUT IF YOU WANT, I CAN TURN AROUND. PROMISE.
I'M NOT LOOKING.
ALL OF YOUR EQUIPMENT WILL FIT INTO THE HIDDEN COMPARTMENT IN THE BOTTOM OF YOUR BACKPACK. THE COSTUME IS MADE OF TITANIUM FIBERS, MANUFACTURED IN NOVGOROD...
...BUT I INVENTED IT! ME, RUSSLAN BOUCHKO! MY SPECIAL WEAVE IS TEAR-RESISTANT. IT IS ALSO THERMO REGULATED FOR COLD AND HEAT.
SO, YOU CAN'T BE TRACKED USING INFRA-RED, AND IT DOESN'T SHED PARTICLES OR DETECTABLE FIBERS. YOU CAN WEAR YOUR COSTUME WITH NOTHING ON UNDERNEATH.
AND WHAT ABOUT THIS R? IT COULD BE USED AS A TARGET. ARE YOU SURE THAT IT IS REALLY NECESSARY?
LISTEN, HONEY. IN THIS COUNTRY, EVERYTHING IS ABOUT ADVERTISING.
YOU HAVE TO HAVE A LOGO!
KEVLAR-REINFORCED KNEE AND ELBOW PADS, BUILT-IN KNUCKLEDUSTERS FOR THE GLOVES.
THE BEST OF RUSSIAN TECHNOLOGY!
EXCEPT FOR JUST ONE TINY DETAIL...

IT'S **NOT** MY SIZE.
I DON'T HAVE ANY OTHER SIZES...
FORTUNATELY FOR ME.

I KEPT THE BEST FOR LAST.
WOW! AMAZING.
YES, YOUR FRIEND RUSSLAN HAS HIDDEN THE FIRE POWER OF A BATTLESHIP IN A BROOM CLOSET.
NO, IT'S JUST THAT IT'S THE FIRST TIME I'VE MET SOMEONE WHO IS MESSIER THAN ME.
?!
I'VE SEEN SPETSNAZ USE THESE IN INFILTRATION OPERATIONS. COOL AND SILENT.
YOU'VE NEVER SEEN ANY LIKE THESE. I'VE REINFORCED THEM WITH MY OWN SPECIAL ALLOY.
THE BLADE AND THE HAMMER ARE MADE OF DEPLETED URANIUM-TITANIUM-MERCURY. PRACTICALLY INDESTRUC-TIBLE!
YOU COULD MAKE A FORTUNE HERE WITH SOMETHING LIKE THIS!
SURE!
EXCEPT THAT OUR APPARATCHIKS HAVE DECIDED THAT "RUSSIAN KGB AGENT" DOESN'T GO TOO WELL WITH "CAPITALIST SUCCESS."
NOW, YOU START TOMORROW, SO FORGET ABOUT THOSE TOOTHPICKS AND TAKE THIS ZS-22. IT'S A LOT MORE EFFECTIVE.
THANKS. BUT NO THANKS.
I'M NOT TAKING NO FOR AN ANSWER! THIS GUN SHOOTS 12.7 ARMORED SHELLS AT A RATE OF 2,000 PER MINUTE. I REALLY CAN'T SEE HOW YOUR TWO LITTLE TOOLS CAN BE ANY BETTER?
THEY'RE COOL.

AS SOON AS I GET OUT OF THIS DAMN CAST, YOU'RE OUT OF HERE...
YOU WILL DRIVE ME WHERE I WANT, WHEN I WANT.
YOU WILL ALSO COOK. AND BE WARNED, I AM DEMANDING! I DON'T EAT ANY OF THAT READY-MEAL CRAP.
BREAKFAST IS AT 7, DINNER AT 8:30, LIGHTS OUT AT 10. AND WHEN I SAY 10, IT'S NOT 10:05!
OKAY.
OKAY.
OKAY.
OKAY.
AND DON'T GIVE ME ANY OF THAT CHEAP SEXING-UP-THE-OLD-BOSS ROUTINE.
IF YOU HAVE SOMETHING IMPORTANT TO TELL ME, SOMETHING THAT IS IMPORTANT TO YOU...
...KEEP IT TO YOURSELF! I DON'T WANT TO HAVE ANY NERVOUS NELLIES AROUND HERE.
OKAY.
YES...
AH, OKAY.
SO, IT'S $70 PER WEEK. THIS IS YOUR ROOM.
OKAY.
WHY DO I GET THE IMPRESSION THAT YOU KEEP SAYING "OKAY", BUT YOU'RE REALLY THINKING "YEAH, RIGHT?"
BECAUSE, NEXT WEEK, I WANT YOU TO COME WITH ME TO THIS NICE MAN'S PARTY. YOUR PRODUCER.
?!
NICE? JOE JONES? WHAT DO YOU USE FOR BRAINS IN ALABAMA?
I WANT TO GO TO A PARTY ABOUT AS MUCH AS I WANT TO PLAY THE BANJO!
WE HAVE TO GO TO THIS PARTY!
AH. AND WHY EXACTLY MUST YOU GO MAKE SMALL TALK FOR TWO HOURS? YOU COULD DO SOMETHING USEFUL WITH YOUR EVENING!
WATCH A BASEBALL GAME!
WHAT DO YOU THINK YOU'LL FIND OVER THERE? A PRINCE CHARMING? A SUGAR DADDY?
OR A PRINCESS! OR BOTH! AND LOTS OF VODKA!
I ONLY DRINK WATER.

THREE FRIED EGGS.
AND DON'T COOK THE YOLK TOO MUCH.
THE MOVEMENT STARTED BY THE "CARPENTER" AND ECHOED BY JACKIE CORE HAS SPREAD THROUGHOUT THE ENTIRE COUNTRY...
JOE EVERETT AND NIGEL FEED ARE BOTH PART OF THE "EQUAL RIGHTS" ORGANIZATION THAT FIGHTS DISCRIMINATION AGAINST HOMOSEXUALS IN THE ARMY.
WITNESSES ARE DESCRIBING A HORDE OF HUNDREDS OF PEOPLE, ALL WEARING PANTS WITH SUSPENDERS, JUST LIKE THE ONES CALLING THEMSELVES "THE DISCIPLES OF THE CARPENTER," THAT HAVE ALLEGEDLY ATTACKED THE HOMES OF THEIR VICTIMS BEFORE LYNCHING THEM.
ARE YOU SURE YOU DON'T WANT TOAST THIS MORNING?
THE COOK
GO BUY SOME FRANKS AND BEANS FOR TONIGHT...
THIS MORNING...
...THEY'VE RUINED MY APPETITE.
THE L.A. PROSECUTOR HAS INDICATED THAT ONLY AN AUTOPSY WILL BE ABLE TO DISTINGUISH BETWEEN THE TWO BODIES FOUND NAILED TO THEIR HOME. THE VICTIMS WERE 21.
WE HAVE TO GO, ALABAMA... I HAVE WORK TO DO...
ME TOO...

SPANK!
SPAN
SEX
SEX
XXX
NIGHTS
WHY ARE YOU RUNNING AWAY, YOU LITTLE WHORE? YOU LIKE TO LOOK...
...STAY FOR THE SHOW!
COOL IT, GUYS. TAKE THIS. I DON'T HAVE A CENT MORE...
THIS DAMNED MONEY IS THE BOUNTY OF PERVERSION.
...AND YOU WANT TO DIRTY US WITH IT?!
YOU CAN BE SAVED! JUST LIKE ALL OF THOSE THAT YOU CORRUPT WITH YOUR PERVERSE IMAGES, BUT WE NEED THE LIST OF ALL OF YOUR CUSTOMERS!
I...I... DON'T HAVE... A...LIST.
WELL, THE DEVIL IS ABOUT TO HAVE A NEW GUEST...

AAAAAAAAAAAAAAAAAAAAAAAAAAAAAAAAAhhh...
BILL!
GOOD GOD! WHAT IS IT...
SHOOT HER!
CAN'T!
TOO QUIC--
POW
I DON'T KNOW WHO YOU ARE, WHORE!
BUT I'M GONNA KILL YOU!
I DOUBT THAT.
AS FOR YOU, YOU'RE GOING TO SPEND A YEAR IN INTENSIVE CARE SHITTING IN A BUCKET AND SIPPING YOUR DINNER THROUGH A STRAW, UNLESS YOU TELL ME WHERE I CAN FIND THE CARPENTER.

...YOU RAT HIM OUT, AND I'LL MAKE YOU A DEAL;
LET'S SAY...
...ONE WEEK IN A COMA AND ONLY TWO BROKEN BONES.
I HAVE NO IDEA WHERE HE IS! AND EVEN IF I DID, I WOULD RATHER CASTRATE MYSELF THAN TELL YOU!
spank! sex
WHAT ARE YOU DOING, VERA? IT'S NOT YOUR JOB TO FIND THE CARPENTER!! IT'S ENOUGH JUST TO BE A HERO FOR NOW!
AND GET OUT OF THE WAY! YOU'VE GOT THE OTHERS, THAT'S ENOUGH! MOVE! YOU ARE NOT FASTER THAN A BULLET!
CLICK
BUT ALL YOU HAVE TO DO IS LOOK WHERE THE SHOOTER IS AIMING...
YOU'RE RIGHT, I'M NOT FASTER THAN A BULLET.
...AND ANTICIPATE.
WHO... WHO...ARE YOU?
HANG ON BEFORE YOU ANSWER! VERRRRRY IMPORTANT FOR YOUR IMAGE! I THOUGHT ABOUT "DEVIL SPIDER"...OR "SPIDER GIRL," OR...
I HAVE ONLY ONE NAME, RUSSLAN, KRASNAYZ DOSHA...
...RED ONE.
spank! sex
Phil's FINE FILM

DAMN WHORES...
?!
LET GO OF ME, YOU BASTARD!
WE'RE NOT DOING ANYTHING WRONG!
NOT... DOING ANYTHING WRONG?!
LITTLE BITCHES! YOU ARE A DISGRACE TO GOD! YOU ARE A DISGRACE TO AMERICA! AND WE ARE THE ONES WHO MUST CLEAN UP.
IT'S SUCH A SHAME TO HAVE INTERRUPTED WENDY AND SELMA...
????
...IT LOOKED TO BE GOING VERY WELL.
DON'T YOU WANT TO LET THEM FINISH...? WHO KNOWS, IF YOU LIKE IT, YOU COULD MAYBE DO IT AMONG YOURSELVES? THERE ARE SOME FREE STALLS.
ARE...ARE YOU CALLING US FAGGOTS?
YES. CLOSET HOMOSEXUALS.
...BUT THERE IS NOTHING WRONG WITH IT, YOU KNOW...

THE PROBLEM WITH BOYS LIKE YOU...
AAAAH!
...IT'S JUST THAT YOU ARE SO SENSITIVE...
AAARGH!
...WHAT AN IDIOT!
LET ME GO...
YOU'RE GOING TO HAVE TO PULL YOURSELF TOGETHER...
AAAAH! MY FINGER...
...OR DIE YOUNG.
STOP, PLEASE! I'LL DO WHATEVER YOU WANT...LET ME GO...
OKAY.
I'M GOING TO LEAVE YOU...
YOU WANTED TO CLEAN UP, RIGHT?

IT'S A SEEDY BROTHEL IN INGLEWOOD... JACKY CORE'S CRAZY FREAKS HAVE DECIDED TO REMAKE IT.
THE COPS HAVE BEEN CALLED. THEY WON'T COME. THE DISTRICT LIEUTENANT IS DELIGHTED THAT THESE BASTARDS ARE CLEANING UP ON THEIR BEHALF.
SO THEY'RE GOING TO ARRIVE "TOO LATE, WHAT A SHAME"...
...BUT I WON'T.
???
WHAT THE...
HUNNGGH!
HUNNGGH!
HUNNGGH!
TELL ME, RUSSLAN...
...HOW MANY WERE THERE SUPPOSED TO BE HERE?
NO MORE THAN THREE OR FOUR...
WHY?

BECAUSE YOU SOLD ME A SOLO MISSION...
...AND I'M GOING TO HAVE TO GIVE YOU A GROUP RATE!
YOU KNOW YOUR PRAYERS?
IT'S THE RIGHT TIME TO SAY THEM? IS THAT IT?
NO, ACTUALLY...
...IT'S ALREADY TOO LATE!

DAMMIT! VERA! CAREFUL WHERE YOU THROW THEM!
AND DON'T FORGET THAT WE'RE GOING TO NEED WITNESSES AMONG THESE GUYS!!
TRY AND LEAVE ONE OR TWO CONSCIOUS FOR THE JOURNALISTS...
"OKAY...I'LL KEEP SOME NICE AND FRESH FOR YOU."
ALL YOU HAVE TO DO IS COLLECT THEM...
YOU DESERVE A TWO MINUTE BREAK, DON'T YOU?
AND A LITTLE CHAMPAGNE...
DO YOU KNOW WHAT TIME IT IS?
ERRR... YES. 7:12PM.
THANK YOU.
I WOULD HAVE REALLY LOVED TO...
...BUT I HAVE TO GO GROCERY SHOPPING.
?!
????!!
?!

Fruits & Vegs
EXCUSE ME, SIR...WHERE IS THE LINE TO BUY CANNED GOODS?
THE "LINE"? I DON'T UNDERSTAND. THERE'S NO ONE HERE THIS EVENING...
I SEE...
SO YOU ONLY SERVE WITH RATION TICKETS. IS THAT IT?
ORANGES $.25/lb
WHAT?
I HIRED A FREAK!
GOOD GOD!
WHAT THE HELL WENT THROUGH YOUR TINY ZOMBIE BRAIN?
IT WAS AN IN-CRED-IBLE STORE, LEW!
THEY HAD SO MUCH STUFF! I COULD BUY AS MUCH AS I WANTED!
YOU COME FROM ALABAMA, RIGHT?
ERRR... YES.
POOR FOLK...

DON'T COOK THE YOLKS TOO MUCH!
AND MAKE ME FOUR EGGS THIS MORNING!
MY APPETITE IS COMING BACK.
IT WOULD SEEM THAT THE CRUSADE OF THE "CARPENTER'S DISCIPLES" HAS ENCOUNTERED SOME RESISTANCE BY THE NAME OF RED ONE.
IN THE LAST FEW DAYS, THE MEMBERS OF THIS NEO-FASCIST MOVEMENT HAVE BEEN DEFEATED BY A MASKED WOMAN, RIGHT BEFORE THEY STRUCK OUT AT LIBERAL MINORITIES.
WITH JUST ONE WEEK TO GO BEFORE THE ELECTION OF THE CALIFORNIAN GOVERNOR, THE CANDIDATE, PASTOR JACKY CORE...
...HAS SPOKEN OF A REGRETTABLE INCIDENT WHICH OCCURRED DURING THE "CLEANING" OF THE COUNTRY, WHICH WAS BEGUN BY REAL AMERICANS.
SHE IS ASKING THE CITIZENS OF CALIFORNIA TO DECIDE FOR THEMSELVES WHAT THEY WANT, AND I QUOTE, "TO LIVE IN A WHOREHOUSE OF COMMUNIST DEBAUCHERY, OR THE TRADITIONAL COUNTRY OF OUR FOREFATHERS?"
WITH UNCERTAINTY IN THE POLLS, JACKY CORE IS CALLING FOR A NEW INTERVENTION BY THE "CARPENTER" AND "AN ALL-OUT EFFORT FROM THE DISCIPLES"...
WHAT ABOUT YOU?
WHAT ARE YOU GOING TO DO TODAY?
JUST THE USUAL, LEW...
...THE OLD ROUTINE.

I'M GOING TO START BY TAKING A LOOK AT THE ADS TO TRY AND FIND ANOTHER PART-TIME JOB...
I'M GOING TO GO SEE WHAT I CAN GET...
...SHOW MYSELF IN MY **BEST** LIGHT.
GIVE IT MY ALL.
AND THEN, TO RELIEVE SOME STRESS...
...A LITTLE **EXERCISE!**
I ADMIT IT, LEW...
...I NEED THESE MOMENTS OF **RELAXATION!**

"AFTER THAT, OF COURSE, I'LL TRY AND LEARN HOW TO COOK A LITTLE BETTER..."
FRANKS & BEANS
FRANKS & BEANS
...AND FOR THOSE WHO CAN'T COOK, WE'LL GET BACK TO OUR LESSON. SO, THE BIG QUESTION OF THE DAY IS **HOW** DO YOU COOK AN EGG?
"WHAT WOULDN'T I DO TO PLEASE MY FAVORITE BOSS?"
BIG HITS IN SOUTHLAN
9 A.M. FINAL
I WOULDN'T HAVE EXPECTED SUCH A WONDERFUL OUTCOME! APPARENTLY, THEY NOW WANT TO MAKE RED ONE TOYS AND T-SHIRTS!
YES... VERA WANTS TO PUT AN END TO PROPAGANDA AND ELIMINATE THE *"CARPENTER."* JUST TO COME BACK TO MOSCOW. MOST PROBABLY BECAUSE OF HER FRIEND'S BABY.
YOU ***HAVEN'T*** TOLD HER THAT...
NO. NOT WHILE SHE IS ON A MISSION. WHAT ARE YOUR ORDERS, COMRADE GENERAL?
WHEN AMERICANS START PREFERRING BOB MARLEY TO JOHN WAYNE...IT'S TIME TO FINISH OFF THE COWBOY, RIGHT?
TELL RUSSLAN WE'RE MOVING ON TO THE SECOND STAGE...
DID YOU BUY THEM READY-COOKED?
CAN YOU GET THOSE?
???
NO.
I HAVE BEEN WORKING HERE FOR THREE WEEKS NOW...THE EGGS ARE COOKED, I DRIVE SLOWLY, AND NO ONE ELSE HAS EVER PUT UP WITH YOU FOR SO LONG.
MAYBE THAT'S SOMETHING TO CELEBRATE...

I LOOK LIKE A PENGUIN THROWN INTO THE MIDDLE OF THE JUNGLE.
SO? PENGUINS ARE CUTE!
WE'D GIVEN UP HOPE THAT YOU'D COME!
I WAS SURE YOU WERE GOING TO BAIL ON ME AGAIN, YOU OLD FOX! BUT I KNOW...NOBODY CAN RESIST THE GORGEOUS GIRLS AT JOE JONES'S PARTIES!
I'VE COME TO PLEASE THE GIRL...
I ALREADY SPEND MY DAYS WITH ALL THESE NARCISSISTIC FOOLS, AND I'M STARTING TO BREAK OUT IN A RASH! THAT'S A SIGN THAT I'VE GONE OVER THE AUTHORIZED DOSE OF EXPOSURE.
LOOK AT THEM! MAN CAN GO TO THE MOON AND THEY ARE ONLY INTERESTED IN TANNING AND FUCKING!
IF ONLY THEY COULD ACT PROPERLY!
WHY DON'T YOU FLESH OUT THE CAST?
HAVE YOU OFFERED MISS ALABAMA THE CHANCE TO SHOOT A FILM TEST?
NO, JOE... I DON'T THINK...
DO YOU LIKE THE MOVIES, MISS?
DO YOU KNOW OF ANYONE WHO DOESN'T?
I KNOW THAT I DON'T MAKE MASTERPIECES...BUT WITH THE SEQUEL TO THE "THE FARM," WE'RE MOVING ON TO THE NEXT LEVEL! WE'RE GOING TO RESTORE HONOR TO SEX!
I'M GOING TO GIVE THE VIEWERS A TREAT, WITH STRONG CHARACTERS, ABSORBING STORYLINES... I WANT EMOTION, REAL EMOTION!
TELL ME, JOE, IS THERE A PRODUCER ON EARTH WHO WANTS WEAK CHARACTERS, IRRITATING STORYLINES AND NO EMOTION?
AH-HA! TELL ME, LEW, IS SHE ALWAYS LIKE THIS?
NO. USUALLY...
...IT'S WORSE.

MR. JONES, IT MUST BE GREAT TO SLEEP WITH ALL THESE PEOPLE...I APPRECIATE YOUR OFFER. REALLY.
BUT LEW NEEDS ME WHILE HIS ARM IS STILL IN A CAST...
BUT WE'RE FILMING RIGHT NOW! IS IT THE SEX THAT BOTHERS YOU?
OH NO.
CHOMP
CHOMP
IT...
...IT DOESN'T BOTHER ME...
CHOMP
...EVER.
I KNOW WHAT I NEED TO DO!
FOXY, SPEND A DAY WITH ALABAMA! SHOW HER WHAT LIFE IS REALLY LIKE FOR A PORN STAR!
SURE...AND SHALL I GIVE HER MY PART AS WELL? AND THEN WHAT?
UMMM... DON'T TAKE IT LIKE THAT FOXY, I JUST WANTED...
...IF YOU DECIDE TO DO A FILM ONE DAY, SWEAR YOU'LL DO A SCENE...
...WITH ME?
UHH...WITH PLEASURE.
SEE, GIRLS! LOOK WHAT YOU CAN DO WHEN YOU MAKE AN EFFORT!
SO WE ALL AGREE ON THE IDEA. WHAT DO I HAVE TO PROMISE YOU, ALABAMA, TO GET YOU TO SIGN UP?
WE HAVEN'T AGREED ON ANYTHING, MR. JONES...AND DIDN'T YOU PROMISE ME A "VODKA FOUNTAIN"?
NO PROBLEM... RIGHT IN THE MIDDLE OF THE POOL...
WHOOPS... IT'S JUST THAT... I'VE FORGOTTEN MY SWIMSUIT...
WHEN YOU'RE AT MY PLACE, DARLING, YOU REALLY...DON'T NEED ONE.

THERE YOU GO, JIMMY, A VODKA GRANITA, NO ICE...
JIMMY...
YOUR DRINK. YOU'RE NOT THE ONLY PERSON I'M SERVING!
SHUT UP, WAYNE...THE CUSTOMER IS ALWAYS RIGHT...
AND THAT CUSTOMER...
...IS A GODDESS.

BEING OLD SUCKS...
BEING OLD...
...OR BEING THE ONE WHO BROUGHT HER HERE?
YOU KNOW... I THINK SHE LIKES YOU.
?!!
FOXY...
...YOU HAVE A BRAIN TRANSPLANT RECENTLY?
LEW...IF YOU DON'T MAKE THE FIRST MOVE, I KNOW WHO WILL...
AND WHERE WOULD THAT GET ME? HUH?
ON THE DANCE FLOOR AT LEAST! COME ON, STOP WORRYING!
COME AND ENJO--
THUNK!
FOXY!!
FOXY! WHAT THE...

...HELL IS THIS?!
YOU WILL NOT MAKE YOUR FILM!!
IT IS AN INSULT TO AMERICA!
"JOE JONES!
"YOUR HOUSE IS A DEN OF LUST, CORRUPTION AND PERVERSION! YOU ARE POWERLESS AGAINST OUR RAGE!
"WE WANT THOSE WHO HAVE SOWN THE WIND...
"...TO REAP OUR TEMPEST!
"WE WANT THE TRAITORS TO AMERICA!
"WE WANT LEW GARNER AND JOE JONES!"
GO UPSTAIRS! LOCK YOURSELVES IN THE BEDROOMS AND WAIT FOR THE COPS!
SORRY, GRANDDAD.
BY THE TIME THEY GET HERE...
...WE'LL HAVE LONG FINISHED!
ARE YOU CRAZY, OLD MAN?
ALABAMA! GET UPSTAIRS--QUICK!
BUT...
RUUUNN!
I MEAN IT!
OKAY, LEW...I'M GOING...

"...BUT NOT FOR LONG."
DIIIIIE!
WITH PLEASURE...
...BUT I DECIDE WHEN!
BIIIIIP!
BIIIP
THAT'S THE LAST THING I NEED!
NOT NOW, RUSSLAN! IT'S ALL KICKING OFF HERE!
THE PSYCHOS HAVE ATTACKED JOE JONES'S PLACE!
SORRY VERA, BUT I DON'T GIVE A SHIT. I NEED RED ONE, NOW.
I'VE LOCATED THE CARPENTER.
YOU HAVE TO GO.
I CAN'T! I'VE GOT TO HELP THEM HERE! THEY...THEY'RE GOING TO KILL THEM, RUSSLAN.
WHAT DO YOU THINK I'LL DO TO THEM IF YOU DON'T OBEY THIS ORDER?

VERA. YOU GET RID OF THE CARPENTER AND IT'S OVER. TOMORROW, HIS DEFEAT MAKES THE HEADLINES, JACKY CORE'S MOVEMENT COLLAPSES LIKE A HOUSE OF CARDS...
AND YOU CAN GO HOME...
YOU WANT TO SEE ALYOSHA AND MASHA AGAIN, DON'T YOU?
SO FINISH IT! TONIGHT!
WHO IS HE GOING FOR TONIGHT?
WHY DO YOU CARE?
WHO?
JESSIE MARYN. LESBIAN, LEFT-WING WRITER AND LEADER OF THE WORLD PEACE MOVEMENT WHICH IS SUPPORTING THE SALT TREATY...
SHE AND HER GIRLFRIEND ARE ABOUT TO GET JOINT CUSTODY OF THE BABY SHE IS CARRYING.
LOTS OF TALK ABOUT IT... TOO MUCH FOR THE CARPENTER...
THAT'S WHY SHE HAD A COP POSTED IN FRONT OF HER PLACE...
HE WAS THE ONE WHO RAISED THE ALARM. HURRY! THE CARPENTER HAS ALREADY STARTED...
NO...
...HE'S ALREADY FINISHED.

"BOOKS DRIVE PEOPLE TO FORGET THE COMMANDMENTS.
"THEY LET THEMSELVES BE LED ASTRAY ALONG THE ROAD TO PERDITION, FOR A LIFE OF SHORT PLEASURES AND LONG SUFFERING...
"BUT, LADIES, I GRANT YOU THAT YOU HAVE COLLECTED SO MANY OF THEM INTO ONE PLACE THAT YOU'VE MADE IT REALLY EASY FOR ME..."
...THEY BURN WELL!

ENOUGH!
I HAD GIVEN UP HOPE OF MEETING YOU, MISS...
A DEVIL IN THE BODY OF AN ANGEL, THEY TOLD ME!
"THEY WEREN'T LYING!
"I'M GOING TO HAVE TO REMOVE THAT SKIN..."
...TO UNCOVER YOUR SOUL.
I'VE MET GUYS WHO DREAMED OF DISEMBOWELING ME... I CAN UNDERSTAND THAT.
BUT MANIACS CAPABLE OF CHURNING OUT SUCH GIBBERISH TO ABSOLVE THEMSELVES...
...NEVER!

MANIAC??
YOU THINK YOU'RE SANE COMING OUT DRESSED LIKE THAT?
OOOFF!
AAAAAAAAH!
A DRESS WOULD LOOK SO MUCH BETTER ON YOU!

"YOUR LIFE COULD BE SO EASY! BUT YOU-- YOU HAVE TO GO AND GET CAUGHT UP IN DRINK AND DEBAUCHERY!"
WHEN YOU COULD BE BY YOUR HUSBAND'S SIDE!
PAMPERING YOUR CHILDREN! CHERISHING YOUR PARENTS AND HONORING GOD!
TELL ME, RED ONE, WHO ARE YOU WORKING FOR? THOSE LOST IN LUST? THE BOLSHEVIKS?
THE BLACKS? THE JEWS?
WHAT ARE YOU DOING HERE?
I CRUSH FASCISTS...
CTHUD!
??!
...AND I LOVE IT!
"...USUALLY!"

YOU ARE A SLUT WITH A COMMUNIST WEAPON...
AAAAAAH!
TAKE IT BACK...
YOUR DEATH MUST BE SLOW AND DRAWN OUT, AS AN EXAMPLE FOR OTHERS.
I DON'T WANT IT TO BE TOO EASY...
HAVE IT YOUR WAY...
HELP ME...
???
HELP ME...HAVE MERCY...
TAKE ME...TO HOSPITAL...
"I AM...PREGNANT."
TO BE CONTINUED...

RED ONE™
A Look Behind

Some of Terry's initial takes on Vera from his sketchbook.

Vera in her "Alabama Jones" garb and finalizing the look of her "'70s" do...

Terry playing around with Vera's character moments and emotions.

Terry's initial designs for Red One's costume.

Playing around with an all-black costume and hammer and sickle elements.

Nailing down the final elements, especially the look of the mask - a combination of the practical and being eerie for alarming effect.

Initial cover before the costume was changed.

Terry realized about halfway through drawing Red One that Vera's black costume didn't make sense in terms of her propoganda mission. She would need a costume that showed up well on film, so a redesign began - going for a more flashy '70s look.

This is the first shot of the revised costume - eventually used as a design for one of Terry's sketchbooks.

On the next page - color tests for the costume. Red was the obvious color choice and made the most sense.

TERRY DODSON
·2013·

Terry's pencils for page 8

Rachel's inks for page 8

Red One #1 Cover Art

Red One #2 Cover Art

A look at how Terry penciled the cover.
The art is drawn on 24" x 18" bristol board.

Rachel's inks over Terry's cover pencils.
She inked the cover with a sable brush and india ink.

TEAM RED ONE (L Terry Dodson, R Xavier Dorison) on a "research" trip.

TEAM RED ONE

Xavier Dorison writes in Paris.
Terry Dodson draws on the Oregon Coast.
Rachel Dodson rides horses.
Clayton Cowles bears with them.

Special thanks to Charlie Stewart and Rebecca Rendon for the color flats and assistance, John Fleskes (Flesk Publications) for design and layout help, Clayton Cowles for finalizing the logo, Google Translate, Laurent Muller for getting the ball rolling, Philippe Hauri and Glénat for making the project a reality, to Eric Stephenson, Jonathan Chan, and everyone at Image Comics, and or course, all of you, dear comrades for supporting RED ONE!

www.redonecomic.com